For Super-Susan-
Vanessa-Penelope-Shoe,
with love
J. B.

To my
Superhero Mum,
with love
T. K.

First U.S. edition 2019

Library of Congress Catalog Card Number 2018961162
ISBN 978-1-5362-0567-1

18 19 20 21 22 23 WKT 10 9 8 7 6 5 4 3 2 1

Printed in Shenzhen, Guangdong, China

This book was typeset in Gaspar.
The illustrations were created digitally.

Nosy Crow
an imprint of
Candlewick Press
99 Dover Street
Somerville, Massachusetts 02144

www.nosycrow.com
www.candlewick.com

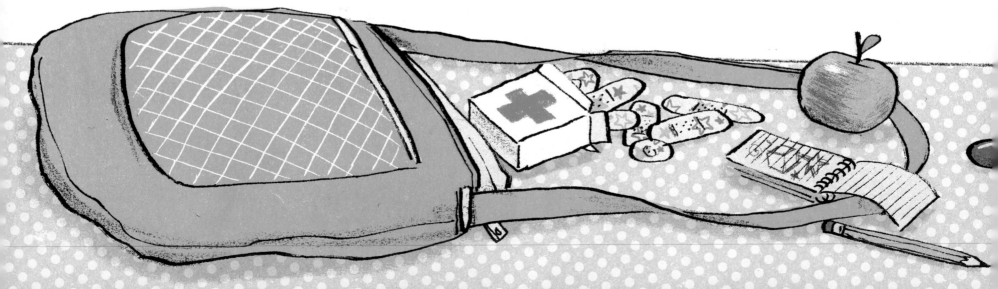

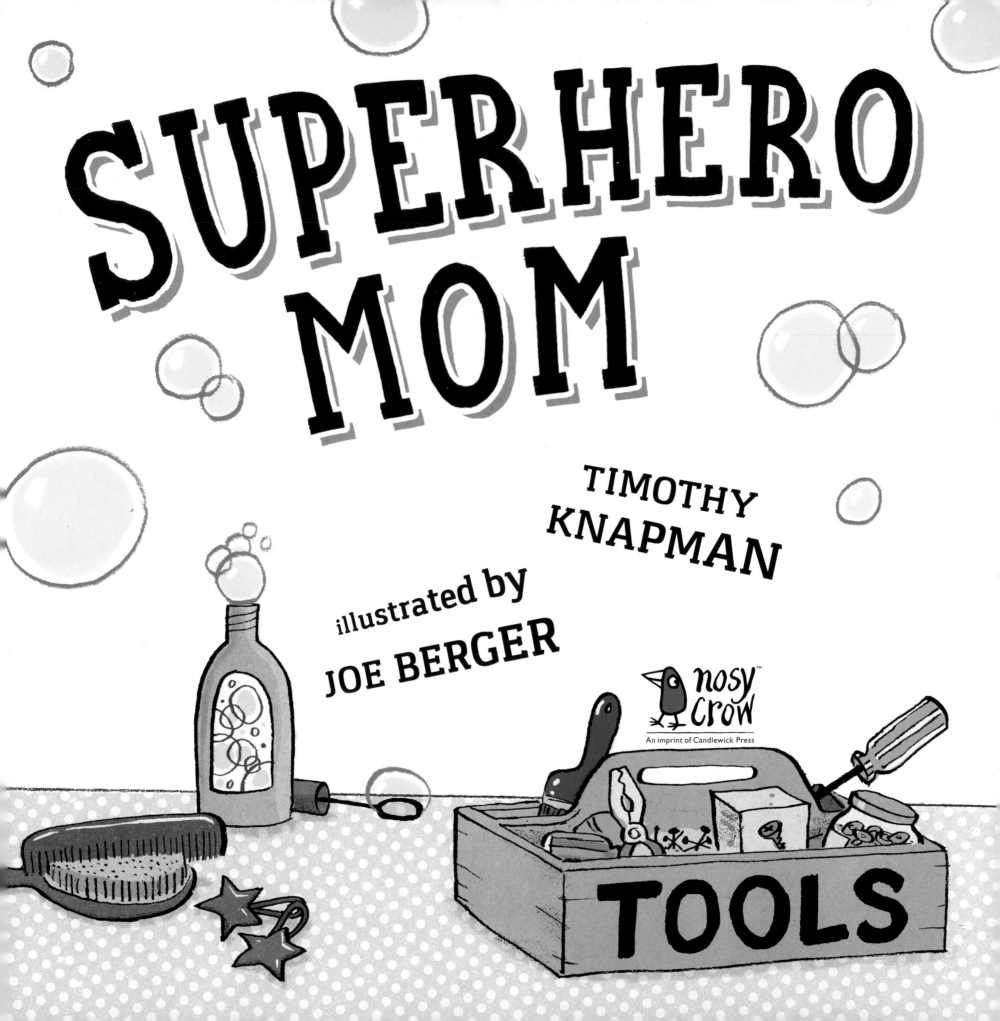

SUPERHERO MOM

TIMOTHY KNAPMAN

illustrated by

JOE BERGER

nosy crow

An imprint of Candlewick Press

TOOLS

All moms are **unique** women, but sometimes you'll come upon . . .

one with a
special
something—
like my . . .

She gets up every morning
with a **superhero leap** . . .

though sometimes even **superheroes** want a **bit** more sleep.

She does so many things at once.
She **ZOOMS** from here to there—

mending . . .

mixing . . .

taming tangles
in my hair.

She must have **superstrength** because she carries **so much** stuff . . .

my scooter,
backpack,
coat,
and even all that's not enough . . .

to slow her when we **run**.
For when I see the bus drive by,
she picks **me** up and goes **so**
fast, I think that she can **fly!**

BUS STOP

She makes up **super** things to do,
like this — my **favorite** game.

(Big Monster Chasing Children
on the Playground is its name.)

If I'm feeling sad because
I fell and hurt my knee,
my mom's the **superhero**
who I **always** want to see.

In a **flash,**
and with a **smile,**

my **supermom** appears,
with a bandage and a kiss,
to **chase away** my tears.

And when I'm playing in the bath,
she makes us both look **weird**
by giving each of us a
really **funny** bubble beard!

She **doesn't** wear a **cape**
or fly to Earth from **outer space**,
but she's the one who **saves** me
when there's trouble I must face.

Like sometimes, when I go to bed,
my teddy **isn't there.**
And I **can't** sleep without him.

"I REALLY NEED THAT BEAR!"

My mom's the one
who **dashes** off
to have a look around . . .

I say, "You are a **superhero** and the **best mom,** too." She smiles and says, "Remember this, my love, because it's true. . . ."

And then she holds me tight and **spins** me in a **super** whirl.

"EVERY mom's a

SUPERHERO

and so is EVERY

GIRL!"